Intoxicate Me

Book .5 of 515 Whiskey Series

by

Tracy Broemmer

Contemporary Romance Novelette

Published by Tracy Broemmer

Edited by Lexie Broemmer

Cover Design: Vanilla Lily Designs

Copyright © 2022

ISBN#: 978-1-951637-44-6

CHAPTER 1

THE QUIRKY LITTLE BLONDE WIGGLED HER BODY AGAINST HIS again. The bar was hopping, and the dance floor was packed, but he'd seen it crazier. She had room to dance; she was coming onto him. Malachi wasn't big on dancing; his buddies had talked him into this. So Roman was getting married? What the hell happened to doing the bachelor party at a strip club? Or throwing a bachelor party at someone's house or a hotel and bringing strippers in?

What the hell had happened to the *bachelor party*? *What the hell happened to his buddy?* Pussy-whipped, that's what.

Aria doesn't want to do the traditional bachelor and bachelorette parties. Aria wants to do a couples' night out. Aria wants....

Sure, Mal liked Aria okay, but he wasn't sure he liked the way she was changing his best friend. Hell, they were too young to do this commitment stuff, weren't they? They'd only been out of school for a year or two. Okay, three. And Roman and Aria had been seeing each other for two of those three years.

Still. Malachi Murphy wasn't about to get caught up in a committed relationship. And he wasn't into nightclubs. Hell, he was a good ole boy. He liked bonfires, boots, Luke Coombs, and longnecks. And country girls with long legs.

But maybe this little blonde would do for tonight.

"She's into you, Mal!" Aria leaned close to him and yelled so he would hear her over the music. Some remix of an old Elton John song. Roman arched his eyebrows as if to say why not? Mal turned on the dance floor, barely moving his hips to the beat. The blonde flashed a smile. She had some moves. Those little hips gyrated perfectly to the beat of the music.

Hell, why not? Damned near all his buddies were dancing with someone. Some of them, like Roman, were caught up in relationships. Some of them just feeling the beat, the alcohol mostly, and the hot curves pressing up against them.

The blonde barely came up to his shoulder. Even in the heeled sandals. Mal took advantage of her spin and eyed her from head to toe. Her honey blond curls were piled in a messy knot at the back of her head. The lacy red tank she wore left her tan, toned arms exposed. Mal had a thing for collar bones and long, elegant necks. The tank stopped at the faded skinny jeans painted on her little hips, still swinging to the beat. The denim molded her lean thighs and calves and led him right down to the red fuck-me heels.

His dick jumped to attention. Maybe he wasn't big on clubs and dancing, but that didn't mean he *couldn't* do it. And damned if her moves weren't sexy as fuck. He could play along. See where it led. The idea of stripping those jeans off her made his mouth go dry. He reached for her hand when she faced him again. She flashed another smile. This one was smaller, less certain. Fuck if that didn't turn him on even more.

Thank fuck his sisters had taught them all how to dance. Maybe not the part about grinding middle to middle, but Breena and Sarah had taught him and his brothers how to move on a dance floor. Didn't hurt that they were athletic and well-built. And apparently, they all had rhythm.

Behind him, he heard Roman cut loose with a loud catcall. He knew his buddy was referring to the way he was now moving with the blonde. Fuck it. He didn't care. The rest of the guys were having a good time; he was going to enjoy himself, too.

If the blonde said goodnight when the dance was over, so be it. His daddy had taught them all to respect women. He'd also taught them all to appreciate the love and loving of a good woman. Mal's parents were still so in love and so handsy, he and his siblings were often telling them to get a room.

Maybe it was the beer making him think so, but the girl could sing, too. Every now and then he heard her butterscotch voice sing out a lyric. Decided he liked the sound of it. Wouldn't mind hearing that voice calling out some four-letter words, his name, God's name—*whatever*—while they did some horizontal dancing. Until then, he threw himself into the groove, circling the blonde, standing close and swaying to the beat, shaking and stepping in time to the music.

Hell, maybe now he would be a big Elton John fan. He didn't dislike him, but his music usually made him think of rainy days. Nothing fun and sexy like this. Mal was still dry; he'd finished his last beer a while ago, and he was in pretty desperate need for another. But damned if he was going to leave this hot number out here to latch onto someone else.

The music changed from the electronic dance song to the slow number all the girls went nuts for in the movie. The one with Lady Gaga and Bradley Cooper. Hell, Mal's mom and sisters could mop the floor with their tears over that movie, and they weren't a whole lot more put together just hearing the song. Mal wasn't into it. At least now he could go grab a beer. Go tell the DJ thanks for the cockblock music.

The blonde had other plans. Before he could take a step —the crowd on the dance floor had doubled when he wasn't paying attention—she slid her hands up over his shoulders and looped her arms around his neck. When the Lady Gaga part started, the blonde started singing along. Mal was mesmerized by her mouth. The idea of those shiny ruby red lips leaving lipstick marks on his dick made his chest ache.

Fuck. He was sweating.

He and his siblings had gone to Catholic schools, being the good Irish family they were. Mal had his doubts about his current dance partner. She was pressed to him like a postage stamp; no room for Jesus or even the Holy Spirit between them. His older brothers had told him bad girls were more fun. Not that he hadn't learned that for himself by now.

"Sing with me."

Mal laughed at her suggestion. He only knew what she'd said because he was watching her mouth so closely, wondering what she'd been drinking. What her tongue would taste like. What the rest of her would taste like.

"Not a good idea." He shook his head.

She grinned, still singing, and loosened her grip on his neck. His dick throbbed again as she smoothed her fingers over his lips. No way she didn't feel his hard-on poking the fuck out of her middle. She met his eyes now as she sang.

Maybe she was a witch, because before Mal knew what was happening, he was singing with her. He didn't even realize he knew the words. But then again, how could he not when his mom had played the song on repeat for a good 47 days after the movie came out?

The slow song faded away and changed to another pop song. Mal wondered if the DJ was drunk with the crazy mix. The blonde backed away a step and started working her hips to this beat—a bit looser and more relaxed, but just as hot as the other song had been. Mal adopted her easy sway, holding the eye contact as he did.

She rolled her shoulders just so, drawing his attention to her tits. Smallish, but Mal wasn't greedy. More than a handful was a waste. Not that he *minded* that sort of waste.

Suddenly, her hand was on his face again. She leaned in close, pressing her tits against his chest.

"My eyes are up here, Cowboy."

If the feel of her loose, soft tits on his chest didn't make his dick feel like steel, her lips drawn up in a little smirk when she drew back to look at him did. Damned if he didn't want in this girl's pants.

"You have pretty eyes." He grinned when he said it. He meant it to sound cool, nonchalant. Might have, but as he stared into her green eyes, he realized she did have pretty eyes. Lined in some kind of purple stuff—yes, his sisters had dressed him up and put makeup on him when he was little, but no, he didn't know what all that fancy shit was that they wore—her green eyes popped. It was more than that, though. More than the pretty light purple stuff on her eyelids.

She looked happy. Vibrant. Like she had stars in her eyes.

Fuck.

Maybe he'd had enough to drink if he was thinking shit like that.

"I like your eyes, too, Cowboy." She nodded. Her fingers were warm on his face. She seemed content to dance that way, her hand cupping his cheek. Maybe she liked the feel of his beard scruff on her hand. Maybe she'd like the feel of that beard scruff somewhere else?

Maybe she just wanted to make sure he wasn't staring at her tits.

"Doin' a toast! Tequila!"

Roman's voice cut through the music. Before Mal could tell him to fuck off, his buddy waved two shot glasses in his face.

"Come over here!" Aria flanked his other side. She grabbed the blonde's arm. Thankfully, Mal's dance partner seemed ready and willing for anything. Mal took the shots and handed one to the girl as they danced their way around a small group to get back to the others.

"To Roman and Ar—"

Aria stepped into the middle of their little circle and held her hands up, one holding her own shot. She shook her head at Kai, the third of their Musketeer group.

"To hot guys!" Aria lifted her glass and looked around at the girls in the circle, the little blonde with Mal included. "To looking and hooking, baby!"

"Woot!" The blonde lifted her glass and tapped Aria's. Mal watched with interest as the blonde threw her shot back like it was water. The flash of pink as she licked her lips sent his blood straight south. Again.

Fuck. She was going to drive him to his knees before the night was over.

The music changed again, and the blonde scooted in front of him, grinding her sweet little ass against his dick. Aria whooped and then she and the blonde were dancing as if they'd been BFFs forever. Mal looked over their heads at Roman, but his buddy only shrugged.

Later, Mal had no idea how much time had passed, but someone had delivered three longnecks to their group since the shot, and he and the blonde had danced to countless sexy songs that kept their bodies plastered together, the girl took his hand and led him off the dance floor.

He eyed her ass as he followed her through the crowd. She had a cute little swing even when she walked. The music now was some sexy country thing by Chris Stapleton. Fine by Mal. Hell, at this point, he was so sexed up for this girl, he would probably stay hard and do her if the DJ played "The Farmer in the Dell."

She led him out the back door of the club. Across the parking lot, someone was climbing into a truck. A few vehicles down, a couple argued about some red-headed bitch. Mal couldn't be sure, but as the door closed and the music faded away, he thought he heard someone vomiting.

The girl latched onto him, her hands hot on his neck as she tugged his face down to kiss him. Sweet fuck, there was no tiptoeing around. She pressed her hot mouth to his, her tongue dancing with his the same as she'd done with his body inside. Sliding. Rubbing. In and out.

Mal cupped the back of her head in his hand and took control. Sort of. She was a firecracker, burning hot and bright, devouring him one flick of her tongue at a time. He smoothed his free hand down her side and dug his fingers into her hip to yank her in tight to his middle. With their lips locked, her soft moan died in her throat. Desperate to taste it, to feel that breath of excitement, Mal kissed a trail from her lips over her chin and her neck. She gasped with surprise when he sunk his teeth into the cords of her neck.

"Take me," she whispered. "Fuck me, Cowboy."

"Here?"

"Yes." She slid her arms back over his shoulders and hooked her fingers behind his neck. "Here. Now. I'm so fuckin' hot for you, I'm dyin'."

Desperate to drive into her and bury his dick balls deep, he slipped his hands under her tank. Her tits were small, but as he thought, they filled his hands just so; her nipples perfectly hard buds against his palms.

"Fuck me," she demanded in a hoarse whisper.

Mal turned and walked her backwards to the brick wall of the club. The person getting into the truck was gone, and the couple fighting had quieted down. Maybe doing the same thing he and the blonde were doing.

"Just a second, Blondie," he growled when she reached for his jeans.

"Let me see it." She rested her head on the wall and stared at him through narrowed eyes. "I wanna see the cock I've been feeling rubbing all over me all night."

"You're gonna have to take your pants off," he reminded her with a small grin.

Eyes locked, the girl unbuttoned and unzipped her pants without hesitation. Mal watched her kick a sandal off as she pushed her jeans down her thighs. No panties. Just delectable creamy skin and a sweet pussy he couldn't wait to sink into. She stepped out of one pant leg, slipped the heel back on, and looked at him expectantly.

"I'm ready, Cowboy."

The throaty whisper did it. Mal pulled his wallet from his pocket and plucked a condom out. Blondie opened his jeans and shoved them down his hips. She took a moment to study his cock straining to break free of the boxer briefs, and then hooked her fingers in the waistband.

His dick sprung free in full salute.

"Sweet God, that's fuckin' beautiful."

Her eyes were on his dick; Mal's were on her mouth. On the tip of her tongue as she wet the center of her upper lip.

"Need you." She looked up at him again.

With another growl, Mal tore the condom open with his teeth and rolled it over his dick. Blondie grabbed his hips. When he stepped closer, she threw her arms up over his shoulders and scaled him like a fucking climbing wall. She wrapped her warm, soft thighs around his hips, the weight of her crossed heels resting on his lower back.

He drove into her hard and deep, thrilled with her look of surprise that melted into sheer pleasure.

"I love the way that feels."

She closed her eyes and sank her teeth into her lip.

"Do it," she demanded as she tightened her legs around him.

Mal dipped his head close to hers and breathed in her scent. The liquor, sure, but she smelled sweet and rich, some perfume probably made to drive guys crazy. And arousal. He could smell how turned on she was. With her tight little pussy clamped around him, Mal moved. Slowly at first. But the pressure of her walls around his dick was too fucking perfect, and he lost control quickly. Pushing. Riding. Pumping. Hands filled with her ass cheeks, his head close to hers, and her ankles locked at his back, he let go and rode her hard.

"Ouch! Shit!" Blondie bucked against him, meeting him thrust for thrust.

"What's wrong?" Mal drew back to look at her. "Am I hurting you?"

"Not you." She stared at him through narrowed eyes, her face frozen halfway between pleasure and pain. "The bricks."

Mal let go of one ass cheek and put his arm behind her shoulders.

"Better?"

"Yes."

Hard to believe that it was the smile that dazzled him at the moment, being that he had one hand on her ass, her naked thighs wrapped around his naked hips, and his dick buried balls deep in her wet pussy. But the smile she gave him before leaning in to kiss him did things to him. Things he didn't get. Things he'd never felt before.

And Malachi Murphy did and felt a lot of things with a lot of women.

She did something magic with her tongue, curling it around his, and then she squeezed his dick with her walls and shoved one hand down the back of his shirt to dig her nails into his skin and the other between their bodies to touch herself.

Fuck if he didn't want to stop everything and watch that. Her small, ringless fingers, the bright red glittery polish on her fingernails rubbing her clit.

"You know how to do this, Cowboy?" She broke the kiss and nibbled on his lip.

"I do." With a flick of his tongue over her lip, he caught her unaware and drove deep in her mouth for a long, hot kiss. "You're killing me with your fingers on your clit, Blondie. I wanna watch that."

"Take your pick." She rested her head on the wall and closed her eyes. "I can get myself off, but I'd like to have that beautiful cock inside me while I do it."

Maybe this was just the beginning, Mal decided. Maybe after this quickie against the wall of Tetra, they would climb into his truck and go somewhere else where he could strip her down and look his fill before tasting her and fucking her again.

He barely held on long enough for her to come first. The brush of her knuckles as she worked herself into a frenzy drove him a little crazy, too. That and the way she tightened her pussy around him again and again, milking his dick. The way she squeezed her legs around his hips. The soft little moans and mewling sounds in her throat as she gave into her orgasm.

Mal let go the second he felt her body tense up and then go slack. He peeked at her when she tipped her head back to rest on the brick wall. She licked her lips and gave him a satisfied smile, still working his dick with her pussy.

"Jesus, Blondie." He dropped his head to rest on her shoulder. "That pussy is fucking perfect."

The satisfied smile jumped to a grin as she moved her ankles and slid her legs over his hips. When her feet hit the ground, Mal let go of her ass cheek and skimmed his hand up her side to claim her tits again. She laughed softly and kicked her sandal off as he stepped back. Feeling like a little kid being told to stop playing and clean up, Mal thumbed her nipple and then dropped his hand and stepped away from her. He plucked the used condom from his dick as she wiggled into her jeans again.

"Thanks, Cowboy." She smoothed her fingers over his lips.

"That's it?"

She tipped her chin to her chest as she zipped and buttoned her jeans. "Gotta go." She looked up with a shrug.

"Go where?"

"Home to bed. I gotta work early." She kissed him. Just a firm peck on his lips. Completely the opposite of the way she'd made love to his mouth when they'd first come outside. "New job."

Stunned, Mal watched her walk away without a word. She still had that sexy little swing to her hips as she walked. Now that he knew there was nothing under the denim, thoughts of laying her down and spreading her open to taste her made his dick throb again.

He didn't even know her *name*. He'd never seen her before. In a town like Long Grove, with a population better than fifty thousand, odds were he'd never see her again.

His dick wanted to see her again. Mal wanted to take her again, slow it down. Play with her hair. Her nipples. Watch her touch herself. His own jeans fastened again, he cupped his dick through the denim and bit his lip before he did something stupid. Like calling after her.

Malachi Murphy didn't beg.

He'd chalk the little blonde up to a fun distraction at Roman and Aria's party. The blonde didn't go inside; instead, she walked around the side of the building without so much as a backwards glance.

Mal squeezed the back of his neck and huffed out a frustrated sigh.

He needed a drink.

The music pounded through his bones when he pulled the back door open. No more dancing for him. He'd go hold the bar down and lift a longneck or two and wait for the rest of the night to be over.

He definitely wouldn't stand there and relive that sweet little piece of ass coming onto him.

CHAPTER 2

EVERLEIGH SHIFTED HER EYES TO THE GLASS DOOR AT THE BACK of the coffee house when she heard it open. A couple of coeds entered, both with backpacks slung over their shoulders. She heard male voices but assumed they were coming from next door where the Murphys were doing some construction work to add on to their restaurant.

Adele Murphy's greeting for the coeds drew her attention back to the coffee house and her new boss and the new job she had started as of an hour ago. The older woman stood with her arms folded over her chest, two silver bangle bracelets visible. Everleigh had met her before, when she interviewed for the job. The woman exuded class with her dark wash denim, the pristine white blouse, and her stylish ash gray hair. The interview had been after five on a Monday a few weeks ago, and Adele Murphy had looked as fresh and attractive then as she did today, first thing in the morning.

Even her dark, plum-colored lipstick had looked freshly applied.

She was nice, too. Everleigh had hesitated at the door the night of her interview. She had driven down from Fort Madison, Iowa, and she'd left a bit late, got caught behind a school bus out on the two-lane highway and showed up for the interview late. Adele had welcomed her with a warm smile, waved off her apology for being late, and offered her an iced coffee.

Everleigh heard the orders, so she went to work filling them while Adele handled the sale. She might have just started at the coffee house, but she'd worked as a barista when she was in high school. The regular black coffee was first. She'd heard the guy ask for a to-go cup, so she filled the twelve-ounce green cup to the brim—he'd specified no room for cream—put a black lid on the cup, grabbed a sleeve, and passed both over the counter to him. He nodded his thanks as Everleigh turned to go back to work on the espresso for the woman.

Behind her, she heard the door open again. The coffee house was suddenly filled with male voices, at least two, she thought, talking and laughing loudly.

"Does Mom know about your hookup last night?"

Everleigh snorted softly and rolled her eyes. Guys would always be guys, wouldn't they? There was a harsh bark of laughter, and then she heard a different voice.

"Why would Mom know, Charlie?"

"Because I heard it from Breena." That was the guy who asked the question.

"What?"

"Aria ran into Breena when they left Tetra last night."

Tetra.

Everleigh froze. She'd been at Tetra last night. She'd hooked up with someone last night. At Tetra.

Her customer was waiting, and now Adele was addressing the guys who had just come in, so Everleigh forced herself to move. She even painted a smile on her face as she turned to hand her customer the espresso she'd just brewed.

There were three guys at end of the counter. All of them with dark, good looks—black hair, bright green eyes, and hard-looking, muscled bodies. And one gaped at her like she was a ghost.

"Oh fuck."

"Malachi Murphy!" Adele snapped. She shot the guys a look that only a mother would use with three grown men.

"Mom knows now."

Malachi—Cowboy, to her—elbowed the one who spoke. The third guy snorted and shrugged at Adele.

"What do you boys need?" Adele still scowled at them, but there was something easy in the line of her shoulders that said she wasn't really angry.

"Just came in for some coffee, Mom."

"And you can get it yourself, Charlie." Adele tipped her head and narrowed her eyes at them.

"Yeah, yeah." Charlie, apparently, nodded. "We will. Just waiting until your customers are out of the way."

The one named Charlie came around behind the counter and grabbed the carafe from the coffee maker. He glanced at Everleigh with a friendly grin.

"Hi."

"Hi." She tucked her hands in the pockets of her denim shorts. Everleigh Johnson wasn't shy. Hell no. Since she'd turned eighteen, she'd lived bold and crazy, no regrets. She didn't regret what she'd done last night. Not even kind of.

But it did make for an awkward morning after to find out she'd fucked her new boss's son behind a local nightclub the night before coming to work.

The third guy followed Charlie to the coffee maker. He reached for Charlie's cup rather than the carafe.

"Getcher own, Sev." Charlie twisted away and threw his arm up to block the other one.

"Can't blame me for tryin'." The third guy peeked around Charlie to grin at Everleigh. "Hi."

"Hi."

Okay, so she was a tiny bit embarrassed now. She didn't regret what she'd done with Cowboy out behind Tetra, but knowing that his brothers were looking at her now and maybe mentally undressing her or imagining pounding her into the bricks—who knew how much Cowboy had shared with his buddies—made her squirm just a little. Especially since now, Adele was looking at her, too.

"You've met my sons?" The smile was slow, but not in a hesitant way. More like the woman was a little too pleased with the situation. Everleigh cleared her throat and nodded.

"Son, yes," she said quietly, taking a quick peek at the one she knew biblically.

"Hey." Cowboy moved down the counter instead of coming around to the back like his brothers. Hmm. Maybe he had regrets? That *fuck bomb* he'd dropped—the one that got Adele Murphy's back up? Maybe that wasn't because he was embarrassed to be caught red-handed. Maybe he had less than zero desire to bump into Everleigh again.

"Hi."

"So." He cleared his throat. "You're the new barista Mom hired."

"I am." She nodded.

"I'm Malachi," he told her. Still watching, Adele harrumphed and finally turned to her other sons, giving them a tad bit of privacy.

"I kinda liked Cowboy." She arched her eyebrows suggestively.

If she expected him to blush, she'd be disappointed. He only grinned and leaned over to rest his elbows on the counter. Maybe he wasn't put off by seeing her again. And if he was, she could set him straight there. Everleigh had no desire to get hung up on one guy; she rarely had sex with the same guy twice. They might have burned the building down last night—worth the scrapes she had on her shoulders from the way he'd drilled her body into that damned brick wall.

But nope.

No, thank you. They wouldn't be repeating the incident.

Ever.

On the other hand, Everleigh didn't just like working for Adele—already. She liked the woman. She hadn't seen her own mother in over seven months. She didn't have much family besides her mom, and her best friend had just boarded a plane for Europe. What the hell was Everleigh going to do here alone while her friend traipsed around Europe all summer?

So, maybe she and Malachi would have to be friends.

No problem on her end. She just hoped he understood the way things would be. She didn't want to have a blemish on her work life right out of the gate.

"You ran off pretty quick last night."

Everleigh mirrored his pose and rested her elbows on the counter.

"Told you I had to be at work early."

"I did, too, and Roman and Aria dragged us all over town."

"Whiner," Charlie said from behind Everleigh.

Malachi glanced at their mother and flipped Charlie the bird when he saw that she wasn't looking.

"Mom, Mal flipped me off."

Mal gave him a double flip off for that, but Charlie only snickered.

"Are they getting married?" she asked him.

"Yes." He nodded and straightened. "Dumbass is taking the plunge."

Everleigh snorted. Okay, maybe she and Cowboy had more in common than she originally thought.

"And on that note, I do need coffee."

Before he could move, Adele's hand appeared between them. Long, elegant fingers. One gorgeous white-gold band of diamonds on her ring finger. Her nails a muted shade of gray.

"Get back to work, boys."

Malachi took the to-go coffee she handed him.

Everleigh watched the three of them saunter back across the spacious building to the door. Malachi turned and took a few steps back toward her. She held her breath, waiting for him to say something stupid.

What if he asked her out right here in front of his mother? When his mother knew something had happened between them? The woman was perceptive; she had to see what was going on.

"It is just Blondie, then?" he asked with a wicked grin.

"It is." She nodded.

"See ya around, Blondie."

If Adele wasn't standing right there beside her, she'd answer him. Call him Cowboy. Thank him again for the ride. Instead, she only smiled, barely holding back a laugh when their eyes locked.

Thankfully, a group of five women came in as the Murphy brothers were leaving, so Everleigh got a reprieve. She had no doubt Adele would question her. But she didn't think the woman would read her the riot act.

And that's what scared her.

CHAPTER 3

"SERIOUSLY?" CHARLIE SHOOK HIS HEAD AS HE REACHED FOR the drywall drill on the floor by his feet. He shot Mal a *get real* look as he picked it up.

"Heavy, Charles." Mal nodded at the piece of drywall he and Sev were holding to the wall so Charlie could hammer it onto place.

"Wuss," Charlie grumbled. He put the drill down again in exchange for the hammer and tapped a few nails into the sheet.

"You that hot for her you can't even concentrate?" Sev asked him.

Charlie snorted. "Hardly. She's cute but too young for me." He slid a sideways look at Mal. "I just can't believe she hooked up with him." He looked back at Sev but threw his thumb over his shoulder at Mal.

"She," Mal emphasized the word, "came onto me."

"Must've been desperate," Sev mumbled.

"Shithead."

Charlie laughed out loud. "Eh, Sev's just jealous, Mal."

"And you aren't?"

"Jailbait." Charlie shook his head.

"Bullshit. She's not that young," Mal argued. "And you're not that old."

"Not to mention you're the one mopin' around, lookin' for true love and unicorns."

Charlie dropped the hammer gently and looked at Sev. "Do what?"

"Heard Mom and Breena talkin' the other day." Sev tipped his head back to shoot a grin at Mal. "They're trying to set Charles up with someone."

"Look, just because I have a heart and want to *use* it, unlike you," Charlie pointed at Mal, "doesn't mean I need help in that department or want to be set up."

"Yeah, tell that to Mom," Mal grumbled. "Or Breena. She's stirring the shit."

"That's right." Charlie nodded. "After all, Breena told Mom about your fling with Blondie."

The three of them headed back out the door to their workstation behind the building where they had sawhorses set up to cut the drywall as they needed it. Charlie and Mal hoisted the next sheet up on the horses while Sev snatched a bottle of water up from a bench and twisted the top off.

"What exactly would she have told Mom, anyway?" Sev gulped some water, wiped his chin with his hand, and then recapped the bottle. "What'd you tell Roman?"

"Nothing." Mal rolled his eyes. He didn't mind the ribbing his brothers gave him. Didn't mind the teasing from his sisters, either, really. But he also didn't discuss the things he did with anyone. Maybe when he was a horny teenager in high school, but he'd long since learned it was better not to share. Saved a lot of women a lot of trouble, and it did go a long way toward keeping his flings as friends.

For instance, Mal wouldn't mind getting to know Blondie better. As a friend. Maybe a drinking buddy.

"He just wants the details," Charlie told Mal.

"Oh, I know." Mal nodded and glanced at his little brother. "You grow out of that eventually."

"Tell me he doesn't mean pussy." Sev stared at Charlie with wide eyes. "Man, I get it if you wanna go all in like Breena and Dan and Pete and Vianne. But tell me you still enjoy pussy when you get whipped."

Mal snorted. "Shut up, Sev."

"Pretty sure I'm gonna enjoy pussy 'til I'm too old or too dead," Charlie mumbled absently as he laid the straight-edge on the drywall.

"Can we stop talking about pussy?"

Charlie and Sev froze and turned matching twin frowns toward Mal.

"Are you sick?" Sev asked him.

"You into her?" Charlie tipped his head and asked at the same time.

"No. And no." Mal rolled his eyes. "But when you talk to her face to face after you get a piece of her, and maybe you're friends, it's probably better not to call it that."

Charlie and Sev exchanged glances. "He's delirious," Charlie said quietly.

"I'll be damned." Sev flashed a grin at Charlie and then turned back to Mal. "Our boy's gotta thing for a girl. Never thought I'd see the day."

"I'm so proud." Charlie played along and laid a hand over his chest.

"I do not have a thing for anyone." Mal pulled in a deep breath, rolled his eyes, and shook his head. "I just think we should have some class. I mean, she's *working for Mom* now."

"Hey." Sev put his hands up in surrender. "We're not the Murphy brother who did her on the back wall of Tetra. Just sayin'."

"What did you say?" Mal pointed his pencil at Sev.

"How'd that work, anyway?" Sev shrugged. "Isn't that a brick wall? Rug burn's bad enough."

"How did you hear that?" Mal stepped closer to Sev and dropped a heavy hand on his shoulder.

"Hear what?"

"That I did her on the wall at Tetra!" Mal snapped. "What else, dipshit?"

"I told you Breena's been talking to Mom."

"I didn't tell Roman or any of the guys that."

"Wait a minute." Bent over the drywall, razor knife in hand, Charlie froze and looked up at Mal. "Seriously? You did it against the bricks?"

"Mom's gonna rip you a new one, dude." Sev laughed and ducked out of the way when Mal tried to grab a handful of his thermal shirt.

"So, Aria told Breena that?"

"Somebody was watching you, bro." Charlie raised his brows and finally turned his attention to the drywall again.

"It's true, then?" Sev doubled over to laugh and backed away again when Mal took a step toward him.

His mother wouldn't rip him a new one, though. She'd just give him that look—the same one she gave him when he was seventeen and she had to come bail his ass out of jail when he was arrested for under-age drinking.

It was a classic combo mom look—anger, disappointment, and a little bit of *try me*. He didn't. Not then. And he wouldn't now. Once your ass was on Mom's radar, you towed the line and then some to get back on her good side.

She would be disappointed in him for the hook-up with Blondie. Never mind the fact that Blondie came onto him. He wouldn't even try to defend himself with that. He was an adult, and in his opinion, so was Blondie, if she was old enough to be in the club in the first place.

CHAPTER 4

"So, you've met my son, then."

Adele had waited for the morning rush to slow before revisiting that topic. They'd worked together with ease, chatting about coffee, their love of coffee, and the weather and everything that didn't make a bit of difference. Everleigh had almost forgotten about the scene with Cowboy—*Mal*—and his brothers.

But when Adele spoke just now, with that seemingly offhanded comment, a little shiver worked itself up Everleigh's spine. She schooled her face into what she hoped was fit for a game of poker and looked up at her boss. She continued to roll silverware; something she'd done in several jobs and could do in her sleep.

"Yes." Everleigh nodded. "I did."

Adele glanced at her as she started another pot of drip coffee. She didn't look angry or disapproving. But there was a tiny little smirk on her face that made Everleigh's belly flip nervously. That look was much more sinister than a frown would have been.

"Malachi might be my biggest pain-in-the-ass kid, and that's saying something." She laughed softly. "I have seven."

"You have——? Seven? Seven kids?" Everleigh gasped. Realizing she must look horrified, she clapped her hand over her mouth. But why would anyone do that to herself? Who would want *seven* kids? At this point in her life, Everleigh didn't even want the responsibility of a dog, much less a kid, much less *seven of them*.

Adele's smirk softened into a sweet, knowing smile as she pressed the brew button on the coffee maker.

"Three girls and four boys." She nodded.

"I'm..." Everleigh shook her head as she did a mental search for a word. Nothing conveyed her feelings other than stunned or shocked, and neither felt like a good thing to say to her boss on her first day at the new job.

"Families were different when Liam and I were young," Adele said by way of explanation.

Not really, but Everleigh kept her mouth shut and simply nodded.

"Well, we were a farm family."

"You have a farm?" Everleigh asked with sincere interest. She and her mom had lived in an apartment as far back as she could remember, and since her mom had moved to San Antonio with her boyfriend a couple of years ago, Everleigh had lived in one little apartment or another. She'd seen cats and dogs and mice, but she'd never been up close and personal with any farm animals.

"Used to," Adele answered. "Sold the farm when we got into the restaurant business."

Everleigh considered that. "You could have kept it. Done the farm-to-table experience."

"Well, we do, but it's not our farm anymore." Adele smiled and shrugged. "Couldn't handle both. Liam's always wanted to be in the restaurant business. And our son Pete is a chef."

"I love that."

"How many siblings do you have?"

"None." Everleigh shook her head. "Just me."

"Really?" Adele's smile slipped; she looked devastated for Everleigh. "Well, goodness. It's good you've met my boys, then."

Right. Because she and Cowboy were off to a good sibling-like relationship. Still, Adele was right. She had no intention of getting that close to Malachi again, but she had nothing against being friends with him and his brothers.

"Was one of them in here earlier Pete?"

"No. You met Malachi—"

Everleigh wished the woman would stop saying that. Did she know exactly what had taken place between Everleigh and Mal? Because she certainly seemed to. The idea of Adele wondering exactly what she and Mal had done made her feel a little creepy, but the thought of her *knowing* exactly what they'd done embarrassed her.

"Charlie and Sev were with him," Adele continued, seemingly unaware of Everleigh's discomfort.

"Charlie and Sev," Everleigh repeated with a nod.

"Charlie's the oldest of the three, but Pete was our first boy. Mal's after Charlie, and Sev is our youngest."

"Got it."

"They're good boys," Adele said softly. Everleigh would swear there was a twinkle in her eyes when she spoke. "They like to raise a little hell, but they're good boys."

The door banged open, drawing their attention across the room. A harried-looking young woman came inside, arms loaded down with books. A worn backpack slung over one shoulder, she hurried to a table, set the books down, and then let the bag slide down her arm.

"Sorry," she mumbled when she looked up and realized they were staring at her.

"Don't apologize," Adele waved her word away. "Looks to me like you could use a cup of coffee."

The woman snorted softly as she approached the counter.

"Can I get that in an IV drip?" She flashed them a worn smile. Everleigh took in her short dark hair and big eyes, but what really drew her attention was the woman's sharp cheekbones and long eyelashes.

"Oh, honey." Adele tssked and grabbed a mug. "Got a fresh pot brewing. I'll pour as soon as it's done."

"That'd be great," the woman said with a nod. "You wouldn't by chance know of any apartments for rent, would you?"

"Shoot." Everleigh groaned. "I just signed a lease on a single bedroom unit."

"Yeah?" The woman rested her hands on the counter. "Any other units where you are?"

"Maybe."

"You're renting down on the corner, aren't you?" Adele asked Everleigh.

"Yeah. In the Sage Building."

"Which way?" the woman asked. "I'm Tatum."

"Everleigh," she answered. "The west corner of the block."

"Great." Tatum nodded. "I'll check it out. Thank you."

"Are you new in town? Or just looking to move?"

"New in town," Tatum answered around a yawn.

"Me, too. Gimme your phone number. Maybe we can hang out."

Tatum rattled off her number quickly, but Everleigh drew her phone out with the speed of an outlaw going for his gun in a shootout. She tapped the number in and immediately texted Tatum so she would have her number, too.

The coffee machine beeped when it finished brewing. Adele filled the mug and pushed it over the counter with care not to spill it.

"Thank you—"

The door banged open again, and the quiet coffee house erupted in bawdy laughter and deep voices again. Everleigh couldn't help the soft laugh when she saw the Murphy boys come in. Tatum, however, sighed and rolled her eyes.

"Adele."

Everleigh watched Adele and Tatum shake hands.

"Thanks," Tatum said again, this time looking at Everleigh.

"Ask Mom," Mal said as the three brothers approached the counter. Everleigh noticed one of them notice Tatum as she carried her coffee back to the table where she'd dropped her things minutes ago.

"Ask Mom what?" Adele narrowed her eyes at the three grown men acting like kids. One of them glanced back at Tatum again and then looked at Everleigh.

"Do you know her?" he asked so quietly, he barely spoke.

"Not really."

He looked disappointed.

"Are you hitting on her?" The third brother asked the one talking to Everleigh.

"No, I am not." He rolled his eyes.

"Can we do the whiskey tastings in here?"

"Now?" Adele drew back like she was surprised.

"No." Mal took a turn with the eye-rolling. "It's an evening thing. Second Tuesday of each month."

"Why here?"

"Well, we can't do it at the restaurant right now."

"Did you just ask Charlie if he was hitting on Blondie?" Mal asked the guy in the middle.

Everleigh met Charlie's eyes with a grin. So, *Charlie* was interested in Tatum.

"Blondie has a name," Adele reminded the three of them. "Perhaps you could be polite and not little heathens and call her by her name."

Everleigh looked from Charlie to Mal with a laugh.

"I don't know her name," Mal told his mom. "She hasn't told me."

"She must not like you then," Tatum hollered from her spot at the table. "Because I just met her, and I have her name and number already."

Adele and Everleigh shared a laugh.

"You can do the whiskey tastings here if you call her by her name," Adele told Mal.

"Which is what?" Sev asked Everleigh.

"I suppose you're going to have to charm her, and she'll tell you if she feels like it."

"Thought you already did that," Charlie mumbled with a glance at Mal. Everleigh snorted but quickly covered her mouth with her hand.

"Charles." Adele tipped her head at him with a severe frown.

"Hey Blondie." Mal moved around his brothers to stand at her end of the counter. "Do you like whiskey?"

CHAPTER 5

SHE STILL HADN'T TOLD HIM HER NAME. NORMALLY, HOOKING up with a hot chick like Blondie and walking away when the fun was over was not a big deal to Mal. But he did usually at least know the woman's name. By now, with Blondie working for his mom, and her sitting with him and his brothers around a four-top table in the coffee house after hours to discuss whiskey, it felt weird. In fact, it bothered him.

It didn't help that she was aware that it bothered him. And worst of all, it drove Mal crazy that his brothers knew it bothered him not to know her name. They'd been sitting around this damned table for the better part of an hour, bullshitting and planning the next whiskey tasting—Everleigh clearly enjoying herself by refusing to tell Mal her name.

"Frankly, Cowboy, I'm fine with Blondie," she said with a wicked grin. She sipped a cup of ice water. His mom had left over an hour ago after closing the place. She had walked Blondie through the motions, though it didn't seem like rocket science to Mal, and Blondie seemed more than capable.

"But you heard my mom," he repeated, aware that he sounded like a whiney kid. "No whiskey tastings here if you don't tell me your name."

With the wicked in her grin toned down to cute and almost flirty, she tipped her head at him.

"Would you even care what my name is if that wasn't your mom's condition?"

A question like that was normally enough to make him sweat, treading into the why-didn't-you-call-me waters. But Blondie struck him as the opposite of clingy. She sat back in her chair, knees drawn up and feet on the seat itself. For a while, she'd sat with her arms looped around her legs, but now, she'd dropped her hands to rest on the chair at her sides.

"I would," he told her.

Sev coughed, but all of them at the table heard his *bullshit*.

"Dude." Charlie looked at Sev with a frown. "Don't be a dick."

Sev stared back with wide-eyed innocence. "I had something in my throat."

"Bullshit." Mal pointed at Sev but looked back at Blondie quickly. "I would. I assume since you're working for Mom, we're going to end up friends."

"That or married," Charlie mumbled.

"Don't be a dick." Mal elbowed him.

"Tell me what goes on at the whiskey tastings." Blondie sounded interested.

"Do you drink whiskey?" Charlie asked her.

"No, but now I want to." She laughed. "You guys are fun."

"All of us, right?" Sev asked with a frown. "Nothing special about Malachi."

"Mmm." She raised her eyebrows. "He's got some good dance moves."

"Why don't you two go on home?" Mal cut a glance at Charlie and Sev.

"Sev, why don't you go on home?" Charlie suggested.

"Sev is an interesting name," Blondie announced. "What does it mean?"

Mal laughed out loud, and Charlie choked on a drink of water.

"I'm the seventh child—" Sev started, but Mal and Charlie both threw their hands out to shush him.

"He is the seventh child," Mal agreed.

"But he's not the seventh son of the seventh son," Charlie continued.

"Mmm." Blondie nodded, but she looked confused. "I know that seventh son of the seventh son is a thing. Folklore, right? Like Sev has special powers or something?"

"Except no," Mal argued, even as Sev nodded his agreement. "Since he's *not* the seventh son."

"But your name is Seven?" Blondie glanced at Sev.

"Yep. These guys just can't stand that I'm special." He shrugged.

Mal threw a balled-up napkin at him.

"Here's our theory." Charlie leaned over and propped his elbows on his knees.

"Oh boy." Sev dropped his head back and groaned.

"He was probably the seventh orgasm of the night."

Mal and Charlie teased Sev with their theory all the time, but hearing Charlie say it now, in front of Blondie, made him want to cringe. Especially since Blondie was now working for their mom.

Her instantaneous laughter chased his worries away. She snorted and wiped her eyes and finally looked at Mal.

"Seven?" she asked incredulously. "What? I just got one!"

Charlie and Sev whooped it up, laughing at him, but Mal held the eye contact with Blondie. Her eyes were light with happiness. She'd been sexy as fuck last night at Tetra. Pretty this morning. And right now, she was cute, being entertained at their expense.

"I could help you out with that," Sev offered.

"No, you can't!" Mal snapped, but he was still laughing.

"Special powers," Sev reminded her with a goofy wink.

"We should just call him *O*," Charlie suggested to Mal.

"Get outta here." Mal rolled his eyes.

"On that note." Sev climbed to his feet and kicked his chair back in. "I like you, Blondie. I hope we see you at the whiskey tasting next week."

Mal and Blondie watched his brothers head to the door, already deep in conversation—as deep as the two of them could get, anyway. Just when Mal thought he and Blondie could talk without interruption, Charlie turned to look back at them.

"Dude," Mal groaned. "Go home. I gotta see your face bright and early tomorrow."

"You don't?" he asked, his eyes on Blondie. "Know that girl? From earlier?"

"The one who clearly was not impressed by you?" Sev asked him. He tilted his head and narrowed his eyes at Charlie. "That the one you mean?"

"I just met her," Blondie answered. "She came in looking like she needed coffee the way fish need water."

"What's her name? Does she live around here?"

"She's looking for a place," Blondie told him. "Her name's Tatum."

"Tatum," Charlie repeated.

"Wait!" Mal smacked the table. "Why will you tell him her name? But you won't tell me yours?"

"See ya," Charlie called. Mal threw a hand in the air to wave at his brothers.

When they were alone, Blondie straightened her legs and relaxed back in her chair.

"So, tell me about this whiskey club."

"And then you'll tell me your name?"

"Maybe."

Mal nodded. "You're gonna make me work for it, huh?"

"Tonight, I am," she agreed.

"It's a growing group—"

"Men or women?"

"Both." He shrugged. "My brother Pete has a great bourbon collection at the bar. At the restaurant. He and his wife Vianne are connoisseurs. They have special evenings in the restaurant. Thirsty Thursday. Cocktails are on sale. Wednesdays are wine nights."

"Let me guess," she said with a little grin. "Tuesdays are tequila nights."

"No," Mal laughed softly, "but I like it."

"I thought the restaurant was your parents' thing."

"Mom and Dad put the money in to get it started. Pete's always been the chef. Dad helps a lot in the kitchen."

"So, your dad is his sous chef?"

"Something like that."

"Go on." She nodded.

Mal liked the way she looked at him while he talked. Liked her thick syrupy voice, too. He'd found tonight that he loved her laugh. There hadn't been much in the way of words or laughter exchanged last night, though he was pretty sure they both agreed it was a mutually satisfying exchange. But he was happy to get to know her now.

She might make a good wingman.

"Pete and Vianne started doing these tastings. They travel some, or their friends do. They have different distributors come in and try to sell them stuff. So, we've started a tasting club. We get together once a month. Talk tasting notes. Decide favorites. Just kind of fun."

"Hmm."

"Hmm? That's all I get?"

She stood and fished in her hip pocket for a ring of keys.

"Sounds like fun," she decided. She backed toward the door, eyes on him. "You have keys to lock up?"

"Yeah."

"My name's Everleigh, Cowboy. I'll see you tomorrow, I guess."

CHAPTER 6

"So." Everleigh topped off Mal and Charlie's coffee. Sev was out back talking to their dad about a problem with the wiring in the new part of the restaurant. In the two weeks that had passed since she started at the coffee house, she'd seen the Murphy brothers every morning. Apparently, it was their routine to stop in and bug their mom, no matter if they were working on the family restaurant or even before, when they worked for their parents *at* the restaurant or coffee house or when they worked other jobs.

Now the routine included coming in to talk to Everleigh. She'd be lying if she said she didn't enjoy it. Having moved to town just a few weeks ago, she didn't know many people. Hanging out with the Murphy brothers was fun, and it was obvious to Everleigh, they were well-known and well-loved around town. If she spent enough time with them, she supposed she would get to know plenty other people and eventually make her own friends.

Then there was Tatum. Everleigh liked her, but the poor woman seemed overwhelmed with stress. She was older than Everleigh, but she was still too young to be so sad and serious all the time. The two of them texted occasionally, and Tatum did find a room at the Sage Building, where Everleigh was living. However, Tatum's little apartment was on the sixth floor, and Everleigh's the fourth, so they weren't exactly neighbors.

Everleigh had asked her once if she wanted to go out for a drink or to grab dinner some night, but Tatum had begged off. Said she was too busy. Fine by Everleigh; but apparently, Tatum felt bad for saying no. Everleigh had found a little potted Gerbera daisy by her door later that evening with a note that just said *Thanks for the welcome, Tatum.*

"So, what?" Charlie coaxed Everleigh now. "I gotta work, woman."

She laughed softly. "I was going to ask Mal if there are any hot, single guys that come to the whiskey tastings."

Charlie snorted, but he ducked his head and lifted his mug to hide behind it.

"Um." Mal blinked at her silently and shook his head. "No. There aren't."

"Kai," Charlie said.

"Ew. No." Mal shook his head. "She's not gonna be into Kai."

"What's he like?" Everleigh looked from Charlie to Mal.

"Like Mal," Charlie told her. "They're good friends. He was probably at Tetra when you—when you met Mal." He cleared his throat with a grin and then ducked out of the way when Mal threw an elbow at him.

"The guy's a tool." Mal rolled his eyes.

"And you're not?" Charlie asked quickly. "When have you ever dated a woman for more than one week?"

"Kelly Dupree."

Charlie looked at Everleigh with a deadpan expression. "That was in ninth grade."

"I don't mind a tool," she told Mal when he looked at her. She quirked a brow at him.

"Obviously." Charlie nodded. "On that note. See you at work, little brother."

"So, you want me to set you up with someone?"

"Maybe." She looked at Mal with a small smile. "That okay?"

"Sure." He nodded quickly. "I'm just not sure what your type is."

"I don't have a type." She collected Charlie's mug and set it in the sink behind the counter.

"Just come with me to the tasting."

"Planning on it."

EVERLEIGH WAS COMFORTABLE AT THE COFFEE HOUSE AND HAD no qualms running things on her own now. For one thing, she'd worked at a diner for a few months, and she'd worked at a coffee house back home for a long time, so she was familiar with all the responsibilities before Adele trained her. Also, she knew if she did have something come up, she could text or call Adele for a pointer or help. She was as comfortable with Adele as she was with the woman's sons, though if she gave that too much thought, it did feel weird.

Still, Everleigh had assumed Adele and maybe even Liam —she'd met him on her second day of the job, and she'd liked him instantly, too—would be at the whiskey tasting. So, she was surprised when Adele left the coffee house before three. She missed their talks; Adele told stories about her kids, yes, but they talked about everything. Everleigh missed her own mother, but this was different. She wasn't trying to replace her mom. Theirs was a tough relationship, and she loved her mom, but she wasn't looking for another one to take her place. Not out of respect or love for her mom, but because Everleigh needed the distance from that sort of authority figure in her life.

Not that her mom had ever been much of an authority figure. Or a disciplinarian. Which was probably part of the reason Everleigh did bad things like shooting tequila with strangers and hooking up with guys she met on dance floors at nightclubs. No, her mother had been more of a friend than a mother, but she'd also been jealous of her and therefore, disapproving and judgmental.

Adele was nothing like her mom in that regard. She was fun. She knew her boys—her kids—weren't angels. She let them have it when she thought they needed it. Everleigh had overheard one such talking to when she'd caught Sev peeing in the coffee house restroom after hours. With the door open.

And yet, she was fun-loving, and she appeared to enjoy her kids and their shenanigans.

That was something Everleigh wished she had: the siblings to cause trouble with and a mom who enjoyed their antics but still demanded and deserved respect.

She worked to a country music station the rest of the afternoon. Adele's choice, not hers, but Everleigh was too lazy to bother changing it. She refilled supplies they would need in the morning. Stacked the menu cards on the counter. Washed the dishes they'd gone through that day and put them away.

Mal and Charlie and a few other guys came in as she pushed the mop bucket to the front of the place.

"Don't do that yet," Mal told her.

"Nope," Charlie agreed. "It can wait until this is over. And then Mal can do it for you."

Everleigh glanced at Mal and laughed when he shrugged and nodded.

"I'll do it."

"Okay."

"Everleigh, this is my friend Roman, and this is Kai."

Everleigh recognized both faces from that night at Tetra. She assumed they knew she and Mal had hooked up behind the building, but she wasn't one to worry about what people thought of her. Not anymore.

"Hey, good to meet you," she told them, giving each of their hands a quick shake.

"Gimme a hand." A new voice boomed from the door. Everleigh looked over Mal's shoulder to see a slimmer, slightly shorter version of Mal step inside, a big box in his hands. Charlie turned to help, but the guy shrugged him off and nodded his head to the door. "Stuff in the truck."

"That's Pete," Mal told her.

"And he's the oldest?"

"Oldest brother."

"God, you all look alike."

"Except that I'm the best looking one, right?"

Everleigh met his eyes and grinned. "Right. Of course."

He was, but then she wasn't the type to tell guys that. She wasn't the type to say much at all to guys she was attracted to. A quick hook-up, a make out session if a hook-up was out of the question and she was ready to move on.

She watched as Pete lowered the box to the table and straightened to look around.

"Hey!" He offered her the warm, welcoming Murphy grin and approached her with his hand out for a shake. "You must be Everleigh."

"I am."

"I'm going to choose to think of you as Mom's new employee."

"As opposed to what?" Mal asked his brother.

"She's too pretty for you, so I don't believe anything your sister said."

Before long, the coffee house was packed. Everleigh was both surprised and impressed by the number of people here. She had assumed this was just a small group of guys with an excuse to get together and drink. But as Pete passed out stapled packets with information on them about the whiskey lineup for the night and Charlie passed out small, apothecary bottles prefilled with each of the whiskeys in the lineup, she realized this was something a bit more involved.

When they started finally, she counted three other women in the room. One of them was probably Adele's age. One was somewhere between Everleigh and Adele, but she didn't appear to be tasting anything. The sour look on her face would have convinced Everleigh, but there was no glass in front of her, either. Maybe she was dragged here to be a designated driver.

Everleigh, sitting at a table with Mal, Charlie, and Mal's two friends, tried each of the offerings. She would have been okay to pay for her own tasting; she wasn't rolling in anything right now, least of all dough. But she could have scraped the money together. But each time Mal tasted his, he passed the glass to her.

She didn't hate what she was tasting—tonight's lineup was Nickolas Baxter. But she didn't know what she was supposed to smell or taste, either. Now that she was here, doing this, she wanted to learn.

"This isn't right," she said with a laugh. She was talking to Mal, but all the guys at the table watched her. "You're supposed to get three sips out of one glass. You're not getting that, and I don't know what I'm doing."

"How about a private lesson?" Kai suggested.

Kai, with his spiky blond hair and pretty boy, clean-shaven face, was hot. If Mal weren't sitting here by her, and if she hadn't hooked up with Mal already, she might find his friend Kai irresistible. But in comparison to Mal, he looked too young, too sweet.

"If Everleigh's getting a private whiskey lesson," Mal said flatly, "it'll be from me."

She eyed Kai for a moment and then looked at Mal.

Oh, she definitely wouldn't mind a private whiskey lesson with Mal.

"And am I getting a private lesson?"

"Of course." He nodded.

When the night was over, Charlie and Mal helped Pete pick everything up. Everleigh offered to wash the glasses, but Pete thanked her and said no, he'd run them through the dishwasher at the restaurant. Mal filled the mop bucket with hot, soapy water and plunged the mop deep.

Everleigh hopped up on the counter to watch him.

"I think we need to discuss my payment," he told her as he swiped the mop back and forth over the floor near the door.

"For mopping? No way." She shook her head when he looked at her. "I said I would do it."

"For the private tastings."

Oh. The private tastings.

"Okay." She nodded. A fluttery little tingle started in her toes as Mal propped the mop against the wall and took a few slow, deliberate steps toward her. "What do you think is fair?"

"Who said anything about fair?"

"Good point," she agreed, the tingle climbing up through her knees and her inner thighs. Mal stopped in front of her, a few feet away. "What am I gonna owe you?"

They were flirting. Not in her usual bag of tricks, not at this stage in the game. But this was fun. She *liked* this. She liked *Malachi*.

Which could be a problem.

"Well." Mal's next move surprised her. He stepped forward but moved off to stand at her side. Everleigh had been ready to wrap her legs around him if he'd stepped between her knees. "I was thinking you would be a good wingman."

"Me? A good wingman?" She laughed softly.

"You're like one of the guys," he said with a shrug. "With the obvious exceptions."

"I'm not sure if I should be happy to be like one of the guys," she tipped her head and eyed him thoughtfully, "or offended. Not impressed?"

"Let me finish," he said simply.

"Please do."

"But the idea of *me setting you up with any of my dumbass friends*, especially Kai, isn't gonna work for me."

"And why's that?" Her voice came out as a thick whisper.

"Well, Everleigh." He scooched closer to her. "I think we have a bit of a problem."

"Yeah?"

She gasped quietly when he trailed his fingers over her bare legs and then stepped inside the v of her knees.

"Mmm." He nodded.

Everleigh held her breath. Did she want him to say more?

Yes.

No.

She had a feeling she knew where he was going, but did she want to hear it? Wasn't it best not to get into a conversation like this? Something about feelings?

But she liked him, too.

And hell no, she didn't want to pay for private whiskey tastings by setting him up with someone else. Not at all what she'd had in mind.

She sighed, relieved when he cupped the back of her head and drew her face closer to kiss her. *This* she could handle. She knew how to do this. Maybe there wouldn't *be* any attraction now. Maybe they'd played, and this attempted kiss would tell them if they would be good wingmen for each other. If they would be better off as friends.

And if not, if kissing Mal still made her burn from the inside, well, then maybe she'd burn until there was nothing left but ashes.

And then they could be friends.

Didn't hurt to find out.

He didn't take time to play, to coax her into a kiss. Rather, his lips were on hers and then his mouth was open, and his tongue was pressing at her lips to open them. Feeling the stab of his tongue somewhere lower, in her belly and lower even than that, Everleigh linked her fingers around his neck and kissed him back.

The door opened across the room, but Everleigh couldn't process the noise.

"Mal, did I leave—oh."

Mal's mouth stilled on hers. He groaned softly, broke the kiss, and turned to look at his brother Charlie.

"What?"

"Looking for my phone."

"Haven't seen it."

"Got it." Charlie snatched his phone from a table near the door. "See you guys."

For once, Everleigh was glad not to be teased about the kissing, the making out. But she was bummed when Mal left her there on the counter and went back to mopping the floor.

CHAPTER 7

"What do I do?" Everleigh watched him with wide eyes.

Malachi nodded his head at the bistro table in his kitchen. Wasn't much bigger than a TV tray. If he had his way, he'd have skipped the table and used a TV tray. But the table was a hand-me-down from his sister Joy after she'd dropped by unannounced one evening with dinner. She'd complained about having to stand at Mal's counter to eat.

"Sit down."

She did. Perched on the edge of her chair, elbows on the table, and her chin propped in her hand, Everleigh reminded him a bit of his nieces back when they were little girls watching Breena make cupcakes and cookies.

"Okay, so, tonight we're going to taste three different bottles of Nickolas Baxter."

"That's what you did the other night, right? At the tasting? At the coffee house?"

"Correct." He nodded as he set two Glencairn glasses on the table. "We tasted six different bottles at the tasting. These are different though, because I don't have the money Pete and Vianne do to buy every variety of every whiskey on the market."

"It's expensive?" she asked, eyes on the glasses. "These are cute."

"Yeah." He nodded, plunked two bottles on the table and then grabbed the third and sat down with her. "Okay, first. Nothing about whiskey is cute."

She flicked her eyes up to meet his, a small smirk on her face.

"Except maybe you," he corrected himself.

"You're kind of cute," she said with a tiny shrug.

"Yeah, no." He shook his head. "Guys don't want to be cute. Guys are tough. Rugged. Maybe handsome—"

"And cute." She reached over the table to cup his chin and smoothed her thumb over his lip. "Sorry, Cowboy. You're cute."

Mal rolled his eyes. "Sexy. Sultry. Like you."

That drew a laugh from the lips he'd been dreaming about since Charlie had cockblocked him the night of the whiskey tasting.

"Whiskey is also not cute. It's sexy. It's an experience."

"Whiskey is sexy, huh?"

Everleigh moved her hand from his face and circled her fingers around the bottle of the Southern Rye.

"Yes."

She looked at him and then back at the bottle.

"The glasses are called Glencairns."

She fingered her glass and finally picked it up.

"Why?"

"I don't know why it's named *Glencairn*, but it's perfect for tasting. It's tapered at the mouth so you can nose the whiskey without inhaling too much ethanol and burning your nostrils."

"So sexy," she whispered as she slid her eyes to his. Mal considered kissing the sarcastic look off her face.

"The bowl gives you a good look at the color of the whiskey, and then the base makes it easy to hold."

"Uh-huh." She nodded. "I can see where a traditional glass could be really difficult to hold."

Mal narrowed his eyes at her, but he couldn't hide his smile. "Are you always this mouthy? Were you like this in school?"

She snorted. "Actually, no."

"Should I keep going?"

"Please." She nodded and sat back. He missed her near- ness immediately. The way her sweet, rich scent drifted around her. The up-close look into her eyes. But now, relaxed in her chair, Mal had a nice view of her slender legs. She stared at him with a sweet smile, and for a moment, Mal was tempted to lift her off the chair and taste her instead of whiskey and change that smile from sweet to satisfied.

"Lesson one. All bourbon is whiskey. But not all whiskey is bourbon."

"Is that a riddle?"

"No. This is serious stuff, Blondie."

"Is there gonna be a test?"

"Maybe." He tipped his head and arched an eyebrow at her.

"And if I fail? Will you punish me?"

"You're making this really hard."

Her eyes dipped down from his face to his fly, where yes, his dick was hard as fucking stone behind his zipper.

"Am I?"

Mal laughed softly.

"Sorry. While I am very curious about what's so hard," she grinned, "I also want to learn about whiskey. So I can impress you at the next tasting."

"Long as you're not trying to impress Kai."

"Kai looks like he should be carded when he buys a six pack for his mom."

Mal snorted and shook his head.

"Okay. What did I say last, Blondie? About whiskey."

"All bourbon is whiskey, but not all whiskey is bourbon."

"Correct." He nodded.

"Wait." She held up a hand. "If I pass the test? Do I get kudos?"

"I think we can do that."

"Okay. Go on." She licked her lips. Mal didn't know if she was still teasing him, but his dick took notice of her tongue.

"The government regulates the business. Whiskey is distilled from grains like corn and rye. Bourbon is a type of whiskey."

"Got it."

"To be bourbon, the grain mix must have at least fifty-one percent corn. Has to be made here in the states. And aged in new charred oak barrels."

"So scotch isn't bourbon?"

"No. Scotch is a whiskey made in Scotland."

"And what about rye?"

"Good question." He grinned and reached for the bottle of Southern Rye. "Fifty-one percent rye instead of corn, though there is corn in the mash bill."

"Does it taste different?"

"Let's try it," he suggested. When she nodded, he twisted the cap off the bottle and poured a bit in both glasses. Everleigh picked hers up, but he touched her hand. "Nose it first."

"Do what?"

"Lift your glass to your nose and swirl it. Open your lips and sniff the liquor."

Everleigh did as he told her, but she quickly pulled the glass away and squeezed her eyes closed.

"It's hard," he reminded her.

"So you said." She nodded.

"*Whiskey*. It's a lot harder than a wine or beer. And rye is more aggressive than bourbon. So, it's gonna burn."

"Aggressive, huh?" She grinned. "Then I might like it."

"Just go slow."

"Really?" She tipped her head and raised her eyebrows suggestively.

"You're gonna get three sips out of that pour," he ignored her flirting, but he shifted on his chair to ease the discomfort in his jeans. "The first one is gonna be terrible. Your body's gonna wonder what the hell you're doing, trying to kill it."

"Okay."

"It'll evaporate off your tongue quickly, so you'll adjust, and on the next sip you'll start to notice flavors."

"What about the last one?"

"You can add a drop of water to it, if you want. Some people like that. It opens it up. Changes the flavor."

"Okay. I'm ready." She nodded.

Mal lifted his glass, too, and nosed the rye.

"Am I supposed to smell bananas? Or caramel?"

"Yep."

"Will it taste like bananas or caramel?"

"Ready to taste?" he asked her.

When she nodded, they both tipped their glasses for a small sip. Mal swallowed his easily, eyes on Everleigh. Those brows shot up again, but she swallowed it fairly smoothly and then sat for a moment, as if thinking about it.

"It's not as sweet as it smells," she finally said.

"Right," he agreed. "Because it's a rye."

"It's spicy."

He nodded again as he reached for the bottle of Sir Nickolas.

"Should I rinse the glasses out?" she asked him.

"Yes."

Mal poured while she rinsed the glasses at the sink. When she returned to the table, she slid her leg over his lap to straddle him.

"I like this seat better." She lifted her chin and studied his face. "That okay, Cowboy?"

"We might not finish this tasting," he warned her.

"Sure, we will." She nodded and turned to look over her shoulder at the bottles. "Hit me."

Mal leaned around her to see as he poured their next tasting. They repeated the process. She remembered to nose her whiskey and how to taste it. And once she'd swallowed it, she decided she liked the rye better.

"What's the last one?" She leaned in and nibbled on his jawbone.

"Nickolas' Sin."

"Mmm." Her soft groan made his heart beat a little crazy. "I'm intrigued."

Again, Mal leaned around her to pour.

"We didn't rinse the glasses," she reminded him.

"I think we're gonna have to break the tasting rules this one time," he answered simply.

Instead of following his instructions this time, Everleigh dipped her finger into her glass and then rubbed it over his lips.

"Right now," she scooted up his lap to grind over his dick, "I wanna know what this tastes like on you."

CHAPTER 8

Sex outside Tetra that first night with Cowboy was an adventure, all the more exciting because of the risk of being caught. This was different, but no less exciting for Everleigh. She'd had her eyes on Cowboy's thick cock, and she'd had said cock buried inside her. She'd had her legs wrapped around his hips and his tongue in her mouth. She'd been eyeing that same hard, delicious-looking body for weeks now. Chatting him up when he came in for coffee with his brothers. While their mom watched and even chatted with them. Hanging out with him a few evenings, grabbing a burger, doing the whiskey tasting.

But now, Everleigh wanted to unwrap this man like a toy on Christmas Day and take her time playing.

He didn't argue when her tongue followed the trail of her finger over his lips.

"I like it that way," she whispered, her words in his mouth when he parted his lips. "Maybe we should try them all that way."

"Not gonna argue." His voice was gruff. Everleigh pulled back to look him in the eyes. The smolder looking back at her made her wet. Mal watched her set her glass on the table and then reach for the tail of his shirt. "We're getting naked?"

"You are." She nodded.

He sat up as she inched his shirt up over his flat belly. Everleigh froze, eyes on the six pack abs, the hard cut V just visible under his jeans.

"Holy fuck." Mouth dry, she grabbed her glass again and threw back what was left of the whiskey. "I've never seen a guy with real abs and a real V."

"A real V?"

Chin still tilted down, Everleigh lifted her eyes to meet his. She stroked her finger over the tops of his V and then flattened her hand on his abs.

"I've been with a lot of guys, but you are fucking beautiful, Cowboy."

Apparently impatient, Mal tried to tug the shirt up over his head. Everleigh stopped him when it was at his chest. She wanted him to beg. Hand still on his stomach, she leaned in to kiss him again. First just a quick little jab of her tongue at his lips and then she latched onto his mouth and stroked her tongue over his, over and around again and again. The friction, his nearness, the feel of his cock pressed between her legs made her whimper with need.

Finally, Everleigh took his shirt in her hands again and tugged it upward. Mal lifted his arms; Everleigh tossed the shirt on the floor.

"I just wanna lick you all over," she said softly. She felt his heated gaze, but she didn't look away from his smooth skin, the wide, thick chest and shoulders, and his dark, flat nipples. She moved her hands over him slowly, learning his texture. The heat in his skin. The hard muscles in his chest and arms.

She watched her hands slide over his shoulders and down over his pecs again. His cock was like steel between her legs, his heart pounding beneath her hand. Everleigh dragged her fingernails slowly over his nipples. Mal's hips shot off the chair, grinding his cock into her again.

"I wanna play with your nipples." He circled his fingers around her wrists, but she shook her head no.

"Not yet."

Everleigh scooted backwards off his lap to kneel between his legs. Eyes locked with his, she worked his button, unzipped his jeans.

"Blondie." He said it like a sigh. Wistfully. Wanting. When she freed his cock from his boxer briefs, she held the eye contact and licked her lips.

"Nobody's gonna walk in on us, right?"

"No." He gritted his teeth.

"Because I won't stop once I get you in my mouth."

"Fuck." He groaned and nodded.

Rather than take him in her mouth immediately, she traced a line from the head of his cock down the shaft. Mal lifted his hips and tugged at his pants to give her access to his balls. Everleigh smiled as she cupped him.

"I bet you taste better than any whiskey."

Her words hung between them until she dipped her head and flicked her tongue over the head of his cock. She hadn't given a blow job in a long time, and she hadn't ever had her mouth on a guy that looked like Malachi Murphy. Sucking his cock felt a little decadent, like she was tasting a little royalty. Eyes still locked with his, she closed her mouth around his head and stroked her fingers up his shaft.

Mal cut loose with a long, low growl and lifted his hips again.

"Definitely better than the whiskey." She lifted her head and popped him out like a lollipop.

"Suck me, Blondie."

She smiled and took him again, this time swirling her tongue around his tip and then sliding her lips down his shaft to work his cock hard. Mal sunk his fingers into her hair, thrusting his hips with her as she moved.

"Blondie!" He gave a quick tug on her hair to get her attention. Everleigh lifted her head and licked her lips as he froze, hips up off the chair, and let go. She watched the cum pool on his abs and finally looked up at him.

"I would've swallowed," she said simply.

"Your turn to get naked."

She stood quickly, peeling her shirt off in one smooth motion. Mal squirmed on his chair, found his shirt where she'd dropped it, and snatched it from the floor. Everleigh watched him wipe the mess from his belly and then toss the shirt aside again as he stood. Anticipating his move, she wrapped her legs around his waist when he swooped her up in his arms.

"Right here," she argued when he carried her out of the kitchen.

"No way." He nuzzled her neck with his nose, the light scruff on his cheeks tickling her. "We're gonna use the bed, Blondie."

"Mmm." She angled her head away as he latched his mouth on her throat and sucked. "Yes. I wanna get in your bed, Malachi Murphy."

His bedroom was dark, just a bit of light falling through the doorway from the kitchen and living area. Still, she looked around the shadows as he dropped her on the bed and kicked out of his jeans and boxers. Standing naked before her, his cock thick and ready for her again, he opened the drawer of his nightstand and retrieved a box of condoms.

"Do I get more than one orgasm this time?" She propped herself on her elbows to watch him when he took one out of the box.

"Do I need to remind you you're the one who ran off that first night?"

"You gonna make me come seven times?" she asked with a grin.

"I will do my best to make you come seven times, but let's not bring *that* conversation into this."

Everleigh laughed softly as she dropped back to lay flat on his bed.

"What is it about you?' she whispered as she unzipped her shorts and pushed them down over her hips.

"You tell me." He hooked his fingers in her waistband and pulled the scrappy piece of denim off her legs. "What is it with you and no underwear?"

"I like to be ready," she answered simply.

"Let me look at you," he ordered her. Without hesitation, Everleigh spread her legs and bent her knees. "So fucking pretty."

"I like you, Cowboy." She propped herself up on one elbow and reached for him this time. "That's dangerous."

"Let's get you naked." He dropped a knee between her parted legs and slipped his fingers behind her to unhook her bra. Tossing the lacy piece aside, Mal cupped her breast in his hand and dipped his head to kiss her.

His hands were warm and heavy and then light and gentle and greedy as he read her body like Braille. Everleigh gave up trying to anticipate his moves and let herself feel every inch of his body pressed and sliding over hers. His hands, yes. The roll and tweak of her nipples at his fingertips. The sting of his teeth on her neck and the curves of her breasts and finally her nipples. The weight of his body on hers, his thighs pinning her thighs to his mattress. The pressure of his hard, heavy cock as he moved and stretched over her to touch and kiss her everywhere.

She wasn't used to this.

The bed. The guy. The same guy two times in a row. Being touched this way. Like it meant something, yes, but also a little like being worshipped. Everleigh didn't allow this kind of thing, but something about Mal, something about this moment was perfect.

If she'd had more of his whiskey, she might think she was drunk. Maybe she was intoxicated by him. Her heart pounded recklessly hard at that thought. But Mal lifted his face, and in the shadows, he met her eyes.

"What's wrong?" He nipped at her lips and brushed her hair from her face. "You just got all tense there, like you don't wanna do this."

"I wanna do this," she assured him with a nod.

"But?"

She shook her head and stroked her hand down his back.

"You make me feel things," she said softly.

He pressed a smile to her lips. "But no orgasm yet."

Grateful that he didn't press her further, because she wasn't ready to think about the things Mal made her feel, let alone *tell him* what she felt, Everleigh laughed and combed her fingers up through the back of his hair.

"Right. I would love to lay here in your bed and come seven times."

"What's your record?'

"For what?"

"Orgasms in one session."

She barked a laugh and wiggled under him to distract him. She didn't have a record. Unless one counted. One and done. That had been her motto since she was seventeen and lost her virginity to her high school crush who turned out to be the biggest asshole she'd ever met.

"You make it sound like we're sitting for a photo session."

"I'd love to have pictures of you like this." He quirked a brow at her. "Naked. My sheets pooled around you. That little flush in your cheeks—"

"You can't see any color in my cheeks," she argued with a grin. "It's too dark in here."

"What's your record? What do I have to beat?"

"I like seven—"

He flicked her lip with his tongue and then nipped hers when she kissed him back.

"Stop it. We are not talking about them when we're naked in my bed, and I'm ready to bury my dick balls deep in your sweet, hot pussy."

"Jesus." She licked her lips. "Please do."

"Number."

"Five."

"Five?" he said thoughtfully.

Five times often, never mind that every single *session* that delivered five orgasms was with her vibrator.

"Challenge accepted." He dropped a kiss on the tip of her nose and scooted backwards down her body. Everleigh moaned softly at the drag of his heated skin over hers. Mal knelt between her legs and watched her for a moment.

"What?"

"I just like looking at you."

She wasn't used to that either. Her first experience with sex had been less than good. In fact, it had left her a little scarred. And the days that followed only made her feel worse. She'd never given a guy a chance to lay with her like this, to be more intimate than a quick hook-up. Mal's attention, his praise, felt good, but she also felt exposed and a little bit raw.

Reminding herself who she was, the things she'd done to put that first disastrous experience out of her head, she lifted her arms over her head and offered Mal a sultry smile. He nodded his appreciation as his eyes traveled over her nude body, posed in offering for him. Everleigh barely held in the sigh of relief when he gave his cock a hard tug.

Before she could speak or even think, he palmed her inner thighs and used his thumbs to spread her open. A soft whimper escaped her lips when he rubbed the pad of his thumb up through her seam and over her clit.

"What about tonight made you wet?"

"I think I'm always wet when I'm around you, Cowboy."

"Good answer," he said with a nod. "But what tonight made you wet?"

Everleigh closed her eyes as he moved his thumb over her clit. Big, slow circles that made her blood hot and thick.

"Um." She lifted her hips, desperate for him to slide his fingers inside her. "Your voice."

"My voice?"

"Mmm." She nodded. She straightened a leg and let the tiny tingles of pleasure ride through her before she tried to answer again. "When you were telling me about whiskey."

"So, whiskey turns you on?"

"Apparently so." She opened her eyes to find him watching her face as he increased the pressure between her legs. "But just whiskey with you. I loved the way you looked at me. When I tasted it on your lips."

"Are you gonna come?" he asked with a smirk as she drew that same leg back into a bend and tried to spread her legs further.

"Please." She covered his hand with hers when he slowed his movements. "Please, Cowboy. Faster."

"Move your hand." He gave her a warning look. "Or I'll stop."

Everleigh groaned and moved her hand to the bed. She twisted her fingers in the sheets as he moved again, and the warm tingly feeling started all over again.

"Malachi." She sighed his name as he moved a bit faster. Finally, forgetting even that Mal was watching, that she didn't care so much about herself as making him desperate to fuck her, Everleigh touched herself. From far away, she heard him groan and then encourage her when she cupped her breasts, but she forgot it again immediately as she pinched her nipples and rode the heat that flooded up through her belly and her breasts and into her head.

"There's one," he whispered.

Too undone—the room was almost spinning, but in a slow, languid way—Everleigh only moaned again and then mumbled his name.

"That's fucking incredible."

She opened her eyes when she felt his fingers in her folds and then the pressure of his fingers moving inside her. Still riding the waves of the first orgasm, Everleigh thrusted her hips against his hand screaming with pleasure and shock when he pressed his thumb over her clit and hit the right spot inside her.

"Two."

"Stop counting," she ordered him, but there was no venom in her words. No energy. Just a soft, barely there whisper, as she struggled to catch her breath.

"Hang on, Blondie."

Everleigh lifted her head to watch him slide off the edge of the bed. Face framed between her thighs, he slid his hands under her and tugged her to the edge of the bed. Everleigh almost balked. She wasn't big on this—again, thanks to her first experience. Not that it had even happened, because he hadn't given a flying fuck if Everleigh enjoyed what they were doing.

Still, it was pressure. Hard to relax. She didn't know how to let go and get out of her head—

Mal probed her gently with his tongue. His breath was hot on her wet, sensitive skin. Watching him now, she saw that his eyes were closed as he licked her clit and then opened her with his thumbs and kissed her folds.

"Mal..."

"No hurry, Blondie," he told her without looking at her. "I love the way you taste, and I can and will eat you all night."

Her body heavy with satisfaction and greed for more, Everleigh lifted her hand and raked her fingers through his hair.

"Do you want me to stop?" He lifted his head to look at her.

"I'm just not very good at this," she whispered.

"Blondie, all you have to do is lay there and let me do the work," he said quietly. "And if someone told you otherwise, then *he* wasn't very good at this."

"What if I can't?"

"Does it hurt?"

"No."

"Then you can't. I want my face right here."

She grinned. "Maybe I should have had more whiskey."

"Maybe." He pressed his fingers inside her again and made a show of pressing his open mouth over her to suck on her clit. "You should trust me."

CHAPTER 9

"So." Mal cleared his throat. "Is it safe to say you like whiskey?"

Everleigh's soft laughter chased goosebumps over his arms. She rolled her head on his pillow to look at him. They'd played and taken a break for another taste of each bottle. Mal had turned his lamp on, so he could see her while they made love.

"Is it that? Or maybe I just like you?"

"I'm okay with that." He flashed her a grin and turned to lay on his side.

"Will all whiskey tastings end this way?"

"Well." He pushed a strand of hair from her eyes and then traced his fingertips over her cheek. "Private tastings maybe. Here. Or at your place. But maybe not at the coffee house or 515 when we shift everything back over there."

"You wouldn't have sex with me in the coffee house?"

"I'd have sex with you on the counter of the coffee house with an audience, if that's what you want." He slid his foot over the sheet until his toe nudged her leg. "But that audience can't include any of my family members."

Everleigh's smile tugged at him in places he wasn't familiar with. Sure, her lips—smiling or not—always made his dick hard. But this smile did something different. Some kind of achy sensation in his chest.

"I like your family," she whispered. "But yeah, I don't think I'd want you doing all these things to me with your mom and brothers watching."

"My sisters, either." He shuddered. "They'd stop me and point out all the moves I did wrong."

"I'd have to argue with them." She grinned and wrapped her fingers around his wrist. "I loved everything you did to me."

"And," he arched his eyebrows suggestively, "you're still here. And I'm on number five. So, I could break your record. And the other record of which we don't speak."

"What're we doing, Cowboy?"

It wasn't the question so much as the way she dragged her teeth over her lower lip when she asked it that made his stomach flip-flop. The sensation was foreign and unwelcome.

"What do you mean?"

"We hooked up at a club." She flopped over to lay on her back and stare at the ceiling. "This is different."

She had him there.

"It is," he admitted. "But I like it, Blondie."

"Me too." She sighed.

"You don't have to sound so put out about it." He nudged her with his toe again.

"The first guy I ever had sex with was a jerk." She kept her eyes on the ceiling. "I crushed on him my whole senior year. When it finally happened, it was horrible."

"I'm sorry." He winced and scooted closer to her. "I think it's like that for a lot of girls. Because of guys like me."

"You're nothing like him."

"I'm not a senior in high school anymore," he reminded her. "I was a dick when I was younger."

"He made it worse by telling everyone he knew that I wasn't any good at sex. Didn't know what I was doing. Didn't know how to suck his dick—"

"But you do," Mal interrupted her.

She laughed softly.

"I was mortified. So, I set out to learn."

"On real guys?"

"Mmm." She narrowed her eyes. "No. I read everything about sex I could find. Oral sex. Anal sex. Every position.

I watched porn. And when it came to finding out how to enjoy sex for myself, I touched myself. Got some toys. Figured it out."

"So, you're self-taught?"

She giggled. "Yeah, I guess so. I decided to be what every guy is dying to do. Make every guy want to fuck me. But I wanted to get something out of it, too."

"As you should."

They lay in silence for a few moments. Mal hated the story Everleigh told about her younger self, but he had to admit he loved the hell out of who she had become—in the bedroom, but also in the coffee house with his mom and brothers and customers, even.

"Does it bother you?"

"Which part of that would bother me?" He scooted closer again and propped up on his elbow to look at her. "That you taught yourself to give an incredible blowjob? Or that you learned what you like by touching yourself?"

Mal found her hand resting on her stomach and pulled it to his groin. She wrapped her fingers around his dick, but the smile she offered him was sad.

"I told you I've been with a lot of guys."

"That doesn't bother me," he said simply. "Why should guys get to do that shit all the time and then one day just stop and settle down? But girls can't?"

"Thank you." She raised her eyebrows and nodded her appreciation. "But that leads me back to asking. What are we doing?"

"I don't know what we're doing, Blondie." He shrugged. Best to be honest with her. He liked the mystery that first night. Sneaking out to the back of Tetra and pounding her against that brick wall. He liked the bold way she'd gone down on him earlier, and he liked her uncertainty when he put his face between her legs.

But he liked seeing her first thing in the mornings at the coffee house. Watching her interact with his brothers— she wasn't embarrassed that his sister had spilled the beans to his family about their hookup. He loved seeing her with his mom, and at the moment, that was too much to think about.

"But I like it." He brushed her lips with his. "And I don't wanna stop."

"If we get past seven, are you going to brag?"

He laughed, their lips pressed together.

"What about tomorrow?" he asked her.

"I have to work." She yawned. "Oh my God, I have to work. I have to look your mother in the eyes and pretend you didn't fuck me blind tonight."

"She'll know," he mumbled as he fell back to stare at the ceiling.

"How?"

"Dunno." He shrugged. "But she always figures shit out about all of us, and we don't tell her."

"Well, then, you better get busy." Everleigh slid her leg over his to straddle him. "You're gonna have to hit eight, so I can brag."

"Jesus, God, Blondie." Mal groaned as she ducked her head to suck on his neck. "Tell me you don't talk about this stuff with my mom. You didn't tell her about Tetra, right? About the bricks? Your shoulders."

Everleigh straightened and met his eyes. "What was I supposed to say when she asked me about the brick burn on my shoulders?"

Mal could have swallowed his tongue. "Fuck." He groaned. "I'm never gonna get hard again. I can't believe you—"

Everleigh threw her head back and laughed.

"Get hard, Cowboy. I wanna ride."

"Blondie—"

"I didn't tell your mom anything about that night," she promised as she leaned over to drop a kiss on his lips. "She's cool, but she *is* your mom."

"So." He caught her wrists and held her still. "Are we gonna keep doing this?"

"I'm trying," she reminded him with a grind against his hips.

"I mean tomorrow. And the day after."

"Are you asking me to go steady, Malachi Murphy?"

"No." He grinned. "Yes. Hell, I don't know what I'm asking, because I don't know what I want."

"Me too," she promised him with a nod. "And yes. Whatever you're asking, my answer is yes."

THANK YOU FOR READING INTOXICATE ME, BOOK .5 OF THE 515 Whiskey Series. If you enjoyed Mal & Everleigh's story, please consider leaving a review on your favorite bookish site.

KEEP READING FOR A SNEAK PEEK AT TASTE ME, CHARLIE & Tatum's story.

TASTE ME CHAPTER 1

Chapter 1

Charlie Murphy needed coffee. *Yesterday*. He'd already guzzled a travel mug full, and when he made it at home, it was strong enough a spoon could stand straight up in his cup. Not that he needed a spoon; he drank it black. Always had.

"Where you goin'?"

Ignoring his little brother, Charlie slipped out the back and headed next door to Murphy's Brews, his mom's coffee house. No doubt Sev and his other younger brother, Mal, were in the add-on to the restaurant ragging on him right now, but he didn't care. Yeah, they'd barely started their morning, and it wasn't time for a break yet. But then he didn't need *fifteen minutes*.

He needed *coffee*.

And just a glimpse of the woman who always sat at the small two-top at the east wall of the shop. He'd seen her earlier through the window where he was working in the add-on he and his brothers were building. Dressed in pale blue leggings and an oversized t-shirt, hair piled in a messy twist at the back of her head, full pouty lips doing their thing—as usual.

Charlie wasn't sure he'd ever seen her smile.

Too bad, since his damned face lit up like a fucking Christmas tree every time he saw her. Thank Christ his brothers hadn't been around to see it this morning, although the day wasn't over yet. The woman—her name was Tatum—was a creature of habit, and she tended to spend the majority of her day at his mom's place. Odds were, he would see her a few times today, get all jelly-brained and his heart would pound outside his chest like a stupid cartoon, and his brothers would damn sure notice that.

He pulled the door open, not sure if he needed the coffee or the peek at Tatum more. He hadn't slept the past two nights. His damned sisters were always trying to make something out of his insomnia, but Charlie didn't have any baggage. Nothing to unpack. No dark memories from a bad childhood or being overseas in the service. In fact, he knew damned well he had a pretty good life. Didn't mean he didn't work his ass off right there beside his brothers every day, but no—no deep, dark drama making him toss and turn at night.

Damned Vianne had to go and bring up that article she'd read about the link between insomnia and Alzheimer's disease. Now *that* was something to worry about. Charlie's paternal grandfather had battled that ugly disease and lost just a few years ago. Definitely not something Charlie wanted to think about in those small, dark hours before dawn.

His sister-in-law meant well. They all meant well, but damned if his family wasn't just outright exhausting sometimes.

There she was. Laptop open on the table, she stared intently at whatever was on the screen. She cradled a coffee mug in her hands, left leg crossed over her right knee. Charlie took a moment to admire her slender, shapely leg. The few inches of tanned skin between the end of her legging and the start of her gray and blue running shoe.

"Good morning, Tatum," he called to her as he crossed the floor to get to the counter. The place was packed, as always. Only one table was open at the moment, and both cozy loveseats were occupied. Two stools at the far counter were empty, but Charlie knew those were the last seats to be taken. He'd sat there a few times for the 515 Whiskey tastings, and the flat wooden seats were hell on a guy's ass after a few minutes.

At the counter, he peeked over his shoulder to see Tatum had barely looked up from her laptop. She rolled her eyes and looked back at the screen. Charlie turned back to the counter with a grin on his face. One day, she would break. She would say hi. Good morning, maybe. He'd make her smile if it was the last damned thing he did.

Then again, she might get sick of him and tell him to take a hike.

Not one to give up easily, he would keep trying. Even if she did tell him to go to hell, he would just remind her hell might be a bigger party than the place upstairs, and that he planned to enjoy himself, no matter where life took him.

"You know you've struck out with her at least enough to have gone through a whole line-up by now, right?"

"You are cruel." He pointed his finger at his mom. "Thought you were on my side."

"Oh, I am," she told him with a nod. "Just not sure you're gonna be able to crack that one."

"What's her story?" he asked the same as he did every morning. Odds were, his mom knew more about Tatum than she let on. And if she didn't, Mal's girlfriend Everleigh did. While their tight lips frustrated him, he was also glad the beautiful woman with the sad face and pouty lips had someone to confide in.

"Isn't it a little early for a break?"

"Ouch." He flattened his hand over his heart and shook his head. "You wound me, Mom."

She tipped her head and glanced at her watch as if to remind him again it was too early for a break.

"I need some caffeine." He sighed and drummed his fingers on the countertop.

"Still not sleeping?"

"No. And Vianne's worries over the link between insomnia and Alzheimer's didn't help that."

"Vianne shared that with you?"

"She did." Charlie nodded. "Where's Everleigh?"

"In the back straightening the stock room."

Charlie watched his mom pour the nectar of the gods in a large to-go cup for him.

"You're not gonna bother her." She made the announcement as she gently pushed the cup over the counter to him.

"Why would you think I want to bother her?"

"Because you do every morning." His mom shrugged.

"Did Dad pee in your Wheaties today?" Charlie pressed the white plastic lid on his cup and eyed her while he took a sip.

"Charles Murphy."

If the *mom* look and the no-nonsense tone didn't tell him she meant business, the finger point did. No telling what had his mom in a foul mood today. Odds were she and

Dad had words earlier, and just as likely, they would make up before lunch time.

"Thanks, Mom." He turned to head back out. Mal and Sev would know Tatum was in here, and they would razz him about having to get his fix. About her blowing him off. Charlie had hoped to see Everleigh for a moment, not just to try and squeeze something out of her about Tatum, but also so he could lie to Mal and tell him he'd flirted with his girlfriend.

Not that Mal would be worried. No one in the Murphy family ever thought Mal would settle down, including Mal. And yet, here he was, seeing a girl he'd hooked up with the night of his buddy and his fiancée's couple's night out. Even more of a surprise—Everleigh seemed crazy about Mal and fit right in with the family.

"Charlie?"

He turned to look at his mom but kept walking backwards.

"Hmm?"

"Have you talked to your doctor about it?"

He felt Tatum's eyes burn a hole through him. Even with her table now, he stared at his mom, stunned by her question and more so, the timing of her question, and wondered if she'd done it to be ornery. He knew she was worried about him, but dammit all, now Tatum was probably sitting here thinking his mom was talking about erectile dysfunction and that Charlie couldn't get it up.

***

Read the rest of Charlie & Tatum's story here:

Taste Me

About the Author

Tracy is the author of several contemporary romance titles, including Plus One, Wedding Day Shenanigans, The Mississippi Queen Trilogy, and the H Books—Gettin' Hitched, Hookin' Up, and Holdin' On. Tracy also writes women's fiction and is the author of the Williams Legacy series as well as several stand-alone titles.

Tracy's books have been called gripping, emotional, and timely, and readers describe her characters as real and relatable.

Tracy lives in Midwestern Illinois with her husband of 29 years.

Find her on the web at www.broemmerbooks.com

Also by Tracy Broemmer

Women's Fiction Novels:

Luther's Cross (10th Anniversary Edition)

Fairytale (Writing as Therese Kinkaide)

Just Like Them

Small Hours

Picket Fences

Two Story Home

Green-Eyed Girl

Say Everything

Come Home for Christmas

Sketching Litchfield Lake

Ever, Again

Safe as Houses

Damsel

The Valentine Suite

Women's Fiction Series in Order

Lorelei Bluffs

Every Little Thing

Two A.M.

Blind

Leaving July

Hesitation Marks

Four Letter Words

See Kate

Loved You More

A Lorelei Ending

I Do

The Williams Legacy

Truth Is

Other People's Ugly

Omissions

Women's Fiction Short Stories

India Falls

Luther's Cross: 87,600

The Candy Cane Tree of Willow Lane

Delays

Same Time Next Year

Contemporary Romance Novels

Destiny's Calling: Your Future is Waiting

Wedding Day Shenanigans

Holiday Fling

The Kiss Off

Something Like Love

Plus One

End in Flames

Contemporary Romance Series In Order

The Mississippi Queen Trilogy

Love, Nashville

Forever, Duncan

Always, Jess

Truly, Dante (A Short Story)

The H Books

Gettin' Hitched

Hookin' Up'

Holdin' On (A Novella)

Timberton Hounds (Novellas)

Priceless Memory (A Short Story)

Endless Summer

Homeless Holiday

Restless Hearts (Currently included in Fall Into Love, an anthology by Fluffy Fox Publishing)

515 Whiskey

Intoxicate Me (A Novella)

Taste Me

Kissing Springs Trio

Shameless Santa

Sunshine & Soulmates

Bourbon & Bedposts

Lockland Distilling: Keys to Love Trilogy & Kissing Springs World

Leaving You (A Short Story)

Seducing You (A Novella)

Kissing You (A Novella—currently included in the Let's Get Naughty, Volume 2)

Shared World Novels

Hold Onto the Stars (Blue Collar Romance Series, Book #5)

The Jane Thing (Meet Cute Book Club Series, Book #2)

Shameless Santa (Welcome to Kissing Springs, Book #7)

Doctor Divine (Doctors of Eastport, Season 2)

Sunshine & Soulmates (Welcome to Kissing Springs, Book #

Bourbon & Bedposts (Welcome to Kissing Springs, Book #

Moonlight in Montreal (The Vagabond Series)

Beach Daze (Flamingo Island)

Christmas & Other Inconveniences (Betting on Christmas Collection)

Love in Motion Duet (Novellas)

Feels on Wheels

Rings on Wings

The Wine Tasting Series (Short Romantic Stories)

Perfect Pictures (Traminette)

Coming Home (Edelweiss)

Save Me Every Dance (Rosé)

Marry Me (Shiraz)

Birthday Wishes (Muscat)

Dad Jeans (Vignoles)

Contemporary Romance Novellas

Boone's Girl

Today, Again

Indian Summer

Dear Jaclyn Perris

Mistletoe Mishaps

Deadman's Hollow

French Stuff

Holdin' On

Toasted

End in Flames

Endless Summer

Homeless Holiday

Feels on Wheels

Rings on Wings

Intoxicate Me

Contemporary Romance Short Stories

Truest Love (Currently included in Show of Dreams anthology)

Swipe for Fangs (Currently included in the anthology
Welcome to Whynot)

Mrs. Bennett

Peppermint Lane

The Principles of Accounting

Strawberry Wine

Love Letter

Sambuca Santa

Truly Dante

Leaving You

Priceless Memory

Perfect Pictures (Traminette)

Coming Home (Edelweiss)

Save Me Every Dance (Rosé)

Marry Me (Shiraz)

Birthday Wishes (Muscat)

Dad Jeans (Vignoles)

Other Novellas

The Devy Man, A Horror Novella

The Keeper's Heart, A Horror Novella

Anthologies

Just Coffee — French Stuff (2020)

Snowed Inn, Vol. 1 — Holdin' On (2020)

Aced, Back to School — Boone's Girl (2021)

Snowed Inn, Vol. 2 — Delays (2021)

Sweet Treats — Peppermint Lane (2021)

Sweet Sprinkles — Same Time Next Year (2022)

Rescue Me — End in Flames (2022)

Fall Into Love — Feels on Wheels (2022)

Cool Off — Endless Summer (2022)

Fall Back Into Love — Rings on Wings (2022)

Backing the Bluegrass — Leaving You (2022)

Kissing Santa Claus — Sambuca Santa (2022)

Let's Get Naughty — Homeless Holiday (2022)

XOXO — Trusting Cupid (2023)

Mrs. Right — Mrs. Bennett (2023)

Tease Me — Taste Me (2023)

Falling for the Boss — The Principles of Accounting (2023)

Ride a Cowboy — Seducing You (2023)

Love and Coffee — Makin' Whoopsie! (2023)

Fall Into Love — Restless Hearts (2023)

Welcome to Whynot — Swipe for Fangs (2023)

Let's Get Naughty, Volume 2 — Kissing You (2023)

Show of Dreams — Truest Love